Bad Hair Day

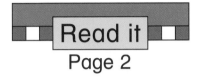

Hare woke up with a smile on his face.

He had a date for lunch, and he was very happy.

Hare put on his robe and went into the bathroom.

"Yikes," screamed Hare. "My hair is a mess!"

So, Hare got his hair wet and brushed it up and down and side to side.

But that did not work!

So, Hare got some blue gel and rubbed it all over his hair.

But that really did not work!

So, Hare put a hat over his hair.

But that really, really did not work!

"There is only one thing left to do," said Hare as he went back into the bathroom.

Snip, snip, snip! "I hope she likes the new me," said Hare.

Knock, knock! Hare opened the door
and looked at his date.

"I hope you like the new me," she said.
"I had a really bad hair day!"

Hare woke up with

_____

a _____ on

_____

his _____.

He had a _____

for _____, and he

was very _____ .

Hare put on his _____

and went into the bathroom.

"Yikes," screamed Hare.

"My _____ is a

_____ !"

So, Hare got his hair

_____

_____ and brushed

_____

it up and _____ and

_____

side to _____ .

But that did not work!

So, _____ got some

blue _____ and

rubbed it all over his hair.

But that really did not

_____ !

So, Hare put a

_____

_____ over his hair.

But that really,

_____

_____ did not work!

"There is only _____

_____ thing left to do," said

Hare as he went back

into the _____ .

Snip, snip, _____ !

"I hope she likes the

_____ me,"

said Hare.

Knock, _____ !

Hare opened the
_____

_____ and looked

at his _____ .

"I hope _____ like

the new me," she said.

"I had a really _____

hair _____!"

Hare woke up with a smile on his face.

He had a date for lunch, and he was very happy.

Hare put on his robe and went into the bathroom.

"Yikes," screamed Hare. "My hair is a mess!"

So, Hare got his hair wet and brushed it up and down and side to side.

But that did not work!

So, Hare got some blue gel and rubbed it all over his hair.

But that really did not work!

Draw it

So, Hare put a hat over his hair.

But that really, really did not work!

"There is only one thing left to do," said Hare as he went back into the bathroom.

Snip, snip, snip! "I hope she likes the new me," said Hare.

Knock, knock! Hare opened the door
and looked at his date.

Draw it

"I hope you like the new me," she said.
"I had a really bad hair day!"

Activities

Read it

Read the day away! Post a daily schedule for your child or student. Each morning, the child can read this simple schedule. Keep your schedule simple by writing it in list format using only a few words for each item. You can also organize it by morning, afternoon, and evening, which ties in nicely with a child's understanding of stories—which include a beginning, a middle, and an end.

Write it

Make your own dictionary! This activity will improve your child or student's writing, spelling, and alphabetizing skills. Label the tops of 26 pieces of ruled paper with each letter of the alphabet. Add a cover page, and staple them together to make a book. Explain to the child that this dictionary can be a reference tool to use when he or she is reading or writing. Each time the child asks for your help in spelling a word, ask him or her to get this dictionary and find the correct letter page. Then, you or the child can write the new word into the dictionary. Over time, each page will become full of words that the child uses on a daily basis.

Draw it

Design a bookmark! All you need to do is cut a piece of paper into a long rectangular shape. Then, supply the child or student with crayons or markers, and encourage him or her to design a personalized bookmark. He or she can draw anything from shapes and symbols to animals and people. When it's done, be sure the child signs his or her name on it. As an extra perk, you can even laminate the bookmarks to make them more durable!

A NOTE TO PARENTS:
When children create their own spellings for words they don't know, they are using **inventive spelling**. For the beginner, the act of writing is more important than the correctness of form. Sounding out words and predicting how they will be spelled reinforces an understanding of the connection between letters and sounds. Eventually, through experimenting with spelling patterns and repeated exposure to standard spelling, children will learn and use the correct form in their own writing. Until then, inventive spelling encourages early experimentation and self-expression in writing and nurtures a child's confidence as a writer.